Garth Pig
Steals the Show

by **MARY RAYNER**

DUTTON CHILDREN'S BOOKS · NEW YORK

For the original Sarah, William, Benjamin, Hilary, Alun, Toby,
Cindy, Sorrel, Bryony, and Garth, not forgetting the original Mr. Pig,
with apologies and thanks.

· ·

Copyright © 1993 by Mary Rayner
Library of Congress Cataloging-in-Publication Data
Rayner, Mary. Garth Pig steals the show / by Mary Rayner.
1st American ed.   p.   cm.
Summary: During a musical concert for charity, the Pig family
players discover that their newest member, a lady sousaphonist,
likes pigs just a little too much.   ISBN 0-525-45023-8
[1. Pigs—Fiction. 2. Family life—Fiction. 3. Musicians—
Fiction.] I. Title. PZ7.R2315Gas 1993 [E]—dc20
92-24508 CIP AC
First published in the United States 1993 by
Dutton Children's Books, a division of Penguin Books USA Inc.
375 Hudson Street, New York, New York 10014
Originally published in Great Britain 1993
by Pan MacMillan, London
Printed in Hong Kong
Typography by Adrian Leichter
First American Edition

1 3 5 7 9 10 8 6 4 2

One day Mr. and Mrs. Pig and their ten piglets decided to form a band. The piglets were all learning different instruments . . .

Sorrel, the viola;

Benjamin, the cymbals;

Hilary, the flute;   Toby, the oboe;   Alun, the triangle;

Sarah and Cindy, the violin;   Bryony, the clarinet;

William, the trumpet;   and Garth, the piccolo.

Father Pig was the conductor, and Mother Pig sang. They played together every Friday.

One evening, Father Pig put down the telephone.

"Marvelous! They've asked us to do a charity concert at the Town Hall."

The next day they all went to the Town Hall to practice.

They played several pieces, then Father Pig tapped the music stand. "I want it to be very quiet here—maybe just the piccolo by itself. Garth, can you do that?"

"I don't know," said Garth. He began very slowly, stopped, then played some wrong notes.

"Come on," said Father Pig. "You can do better than that."

"I can do it," said Toby. "Let me do it."

"Shhh," said Sorrel. "Let him try." This time Garth got it right.

The next number was the one Mrs. Pig was going to sing. They had only just begun when Mr. Pig stopped them.

Mrs. Pig broke off. "Now what's the matter?"

"It doesn't sound right," said Father Pig. They began again. Mr. Pig shut his eyes, listening hard, then he did a little skip. "Got it! It's too shrill. There are too many high instruments. We need something booming away underneath."

"But we're too small to play the big, deep things," said William.

"I've got an idea," said Father Pig.

That evening he wrote an advertisement for the local paper. The following Thursday, when it was delivered, the piglets crowded around to see if their ad was in it.

"Look," said William, and there it was.

WANTED FOR THE PIG PLAYERS:
Cello or double bass or tuba player

All day they waited for the phone to ring.

"Oh dear," said Mrs. Pig. "Perhaps we should have said we'd pay."

"Nobody's paying *us*," said Mr. Pig. "We're doing it for charity. We just need someone who likes pigs."

The day of the concert came, but still no one had offered to play with them.

Mother Pig said, "Never mind, we'll just have to do without. Now, put on your best clothes, everyone. It's time to go."

The piglets scattered. Mrs. Pig ran around finding their clothes, while Mr. Pig piled all the instruments together in the hall. In the middle of this, the bell rang.

Father Pig went to the door. The first thing he saw was an enormous black case. Half-hidden behind it was a lady. "What's that?" he asked her.

"It's a sousaphone," said the lady. "The biggest, deepest tuba there is. I saw your ad."

"Wonderful! But do you know we can't pay you? It's for charity. You'd be helping pigs."

"I'll do it for free. It's a chance I wouldn't miss for anything," said the lady. "Nothing I like better than a helping of pig."

Father Pig looked quickly for her music in the pile. "Here you are. You're in the nick of time. Go straight down to the Town Hall and join us there. You can go *oompah oompah* at the back."

"Thanks," said the lady. "See you there."

Mr. Pig shut the door, ran upstairs, and squeezed into his very best suit. Mrs. Pig had to help him, it was so tight, but at last they all left for the Town Hall.

Breathless with excitement, the Pig family waited backstage. Benjamin ran to peep through the curtain at the hall. "It's packed. I can't see an empty seat anywhere."

"Help," said Garth. "I'm scared. I feel sick. How will I know when to play?"

"It'll be all right," said William. "Here, have a peppermint."

Father Pig said, "All you have to do is keep your eyes on me. And the rest of you, do the same."

They could hear the Mayor making an announcement. Then Mr. Pig said, "Now, follow me," and they all filed out onto the stage.

Mrs. Pig sat on a chair to one side. Father Pig stood out in front. Sarah and Cindy tuned their violins.

Garth and William heard a chair scrape behind them and saw that the sousaphonist was in the back row, her music propped in front of her. She was looking around and licking her lips with a long pink tongue.

Funny, thought William. Must have something to do with how you play the sousaphone. But Mr. Pig was tapping with his baton, and they all turned around again.

The music began. The piglets were in top form. They played three pieces, and after each one everybody clapped loudly.

Then it was time for Mrs. Pig to sing. She stood up and went out in front.

Garth was tootling away on his piccolo, and William filled his cheeks and blew his trumpet, enjoying the deep *oompah oompah* coming from behind him.

Mrs. Pig's voice soared upward, *trala lala LAAA . . .* William cocked his ear. The *oompahs* had stopped. Was that a muffled squeak?

William stopped blowing and, against orders, took his eyes off his father. Where was Garth? Beside William was an empty place, and a piccolo.

William's heart thumped, but he turned back toward the conductor as if nothing had happened. His mother was singing the next verse. His mind raced.

He laid down his trumpet, dropped on all fours, and crept behind the chairs, out of the band. He trotted to the front and tapped Father Pig on the back. Then he reached forward for the baton. Mr. Pig was so surprised that he handed it over without a word. Mrs. Pig, performer to the tip of her tail, kept on singing.

And the band kept on playing. William beat time, drawing himself up as tall as he could. He could see that the sousaphone player was still there, but he could hear no *oompahs.* She was only pretending to play.

Mrs. Pig's song was nearly finished. William could see the sousaphone player getting ready to escape. The band was playing the last notes.

Raising his arms, William took his brothers and sisters straight into the next piece, not giving anybody a chance to clap. The sousaphone player was trapped. She had to stay put. William went on conducting until they reached the moment for the piccolo solo, and then, with a flick of his wrist, he silenced the entire band and pointed *at the sousaphone player.*

It was the signal for her to play alone.

The whole hall was still. Not a cough, not a whisper, not a rustle. The sousaphonist turned scarlet—you could see through her fur. She *had* to blow.

There was a deafening blast, and out shot Garth Pig from the top of her sousaphone, high into the air. He landed on all fours out front, center stage.

The rest of the Pig family was dumbfounded.

But the audience thought it was part of the act, and there was a
thunder of applause.

William swung around and bowed.

"Again!" shouted everybody. "Encore!"

But the sousaphone player leapt to her feet, crashed along the row of chairs, and fled out of the hall, leaving her instrument on the floor.

The Mayor jumped onto the stage and took her place, and the piglets finished their concert with a rousing final chorus.

When they counted the money afterward, they found that they had broken all records.

And in the local paper the following week, Garth Pig's performance made headline news.

As for the sousaphone player, nothing was heard of her for a very long time.